BIG BAD BUNNY

Alan Durant ✣ illustrated by Guy Parker-Rees

ORCHARD BOOKS

For Josie, whose idea this was
A.D.
To Bun in the oven and Bun's Mum
G.P-R.

ORCHARD BOOKS
96 Leonard Street, London EC2A 4XD
Orchard Books Australia
14 Mars Road, Lane Cove, NSW 2066
1 84121 743 3
First published in Great Britain in 2000
Text © Alan Durant 2000
Illustrations © Guy Parker-Rees 2000
The right of Alan Durant to be identified as the author and
Guy Parker-Rees to be identified as the illustrator
of this work has been asserted by them in accordance
with the Copyright, Designs and Patents Act 1988.
A CIP catalogue record for this book is available from the British Library.
2 4 6 8 10 9 7 5 3 1
Printed in Hong Kong / China

Here comes Big Bad Bunny.
He's coming to get your money!

Down the road goes
Big Bad Bunny.
He sees Little Chick.

"Little Chick, give me your money!"
cries Big Bad Bunny.

But Little Chick hasn't got any money.
All she has is a little bit of corn.
"I'll take that!" cries Big Bad Bunny.
Then off he goes to get some money.

Down the road goes Big Bad Bunny.
He sees Little Squirrel.
"Little Squirrel, give me your money!"
cries Big Bad Bunny.

But Little Squirrel hasn't got any money.
All he has is one little nut.

"I'll take that!" cries Big Bad Bunny.
Then off he goes to get some money.

But Little Goat hasn't got any money.
All he has is a little drop of milk.

"I'll take that!" cries Big Bad Bunny.
Then off he goes to get some money.

FROM BIG BAD BUNNY?

Into town goes Big Bad Bunny.
He *wants* to get some money.

Into the bank goes Big Bad Bunny.
He's *going* to get some money.

At the counter is Wise Old Bunny.
"Give me your money!" cries Big Bad Bunny.
"I want it all. I want it now!"

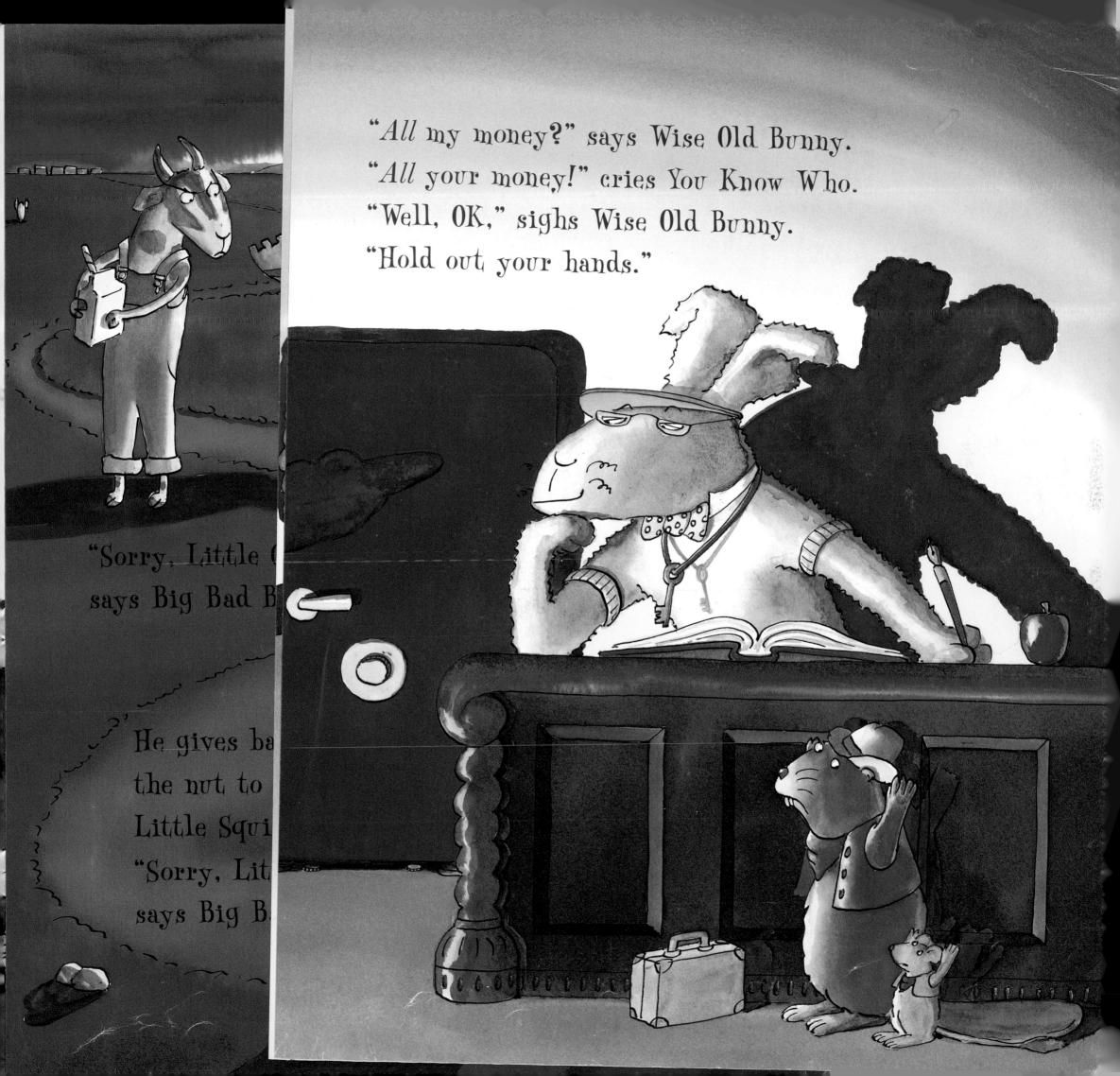

"Sorry, Little G
says Big Bad B

He gives ba
the nut to
Little Squi
"Sorry, Lit
says Big B

"*All* my money?" says Wise Old Bunny.
"*All* your money!" cries You Know Who.
"Well, OK," sighs Wise Old Bunny.
"Hold out your hands."

"Let me out!"
"If you want t
"you must giv
And promise r

"OK, I promi

Everyone is safe now — so is their money,
but things are QUIET with no Big Bad Bunny.

"But, hey, what's this?"
says Wise Old Bunny.